Oklahoma Bride

A Western Historical Romance

By

Kat Lynne

Introduction

I want to thank you and congratulate you for downloading the book, *Oklahoma Bride*

This book is a work of fiction.

Thanks again for downloading this book, I hope you enjoy it!

Table of Contents

CHAPTER 1

R ebecca fought back a cough, uselessly waving her hand before her to disperse the particles of dust currently filling the small room. She gave another shake of the cloth before carefully folding it and setting it aside. She surveyed the small yet livable room with a sigh of satisfaction. After months of scrupulous planning, she was free at last.

The young Rebecca hailed from an affluent family in Virginia, a family that surely was disgraced to have a daughter unwed at the age of twenty. Most, if not all, girls of her age were already in the process of growing their family. She knew of three other girls her age, and one younger, that were already with child upon her leaving. It had been many months since that day. They had undoubtedly already given birth.

Mother and Father had been less than pleased upon learning of her intentions. Her mother desired nothing less than a husband and children for Rebecca. She would settle for nothing else. Father, on the other hand, seemed more levelheaded about the entire situation. They had spoken well into the night on the matter. By the break of dawn, an agreement had been made. They would allow her to make the journey if and only if she agreed to take her eldest sister Helena with her.

Helena had utterly refused. Heavily pregnant with her first child, it was not her wish to raise said child in a strange land where she knew not one person. Mother pointed out the obvious flaw with her not wishing to go. Should she decide to remain in Virginia, she would be faced with the task of raising her child alone.

Her husband had passed the previous winter from an unknown illness. His family would be of no help to her. They had made that point quite clear the moment the two were married. They considered her not worthy of their only son. They had cut the young man off from the will, denying the newlywed couple any help from them.

The pair had been residing within her family home since their marriage. The young man was forced into the workforce, something he had never done before. Father had generously hired him on to work as his new foreman. The young man, Edward, had a knack with horses. Rebecca had grown fond of him.

"Rebecca, oh what were you thinking?" Helena's disapproving tone cut into her reflection. Her heavily with child sister stood just against the wall, hands cradling her stomach, "We shan't survive!"

Rebecca paused a moment. She did not blame her sister for her worry. Her employer had not anticipated two women to make the trip. The place she would call home over the next few years consisted of a small bedroom, big enough for just one person, a small kitchen and a decent sized common area. They would be hard pressed to find space for the babe once it was born. Perhaps the local inn had a room for the expectant mother. It would be something worth discussing with Helena...but perhaps later, when her mood had improved.

"We shall be fine, dearest sister." Rebecca assured.

Helena's lips tilted into a frown, the crease between her eyebrows deepening "I still cannot fathom why mother and father would agree to this...much less forcing me to come along."

Rebecca could not fight the smile that touched her lips. She held great affection for the eldest of her sisters, but she was considered what many would call an acquired taste. Rebecca could not fathom how on earth she had managed to marry with a tongue as sharp as hers. Though small in stature, Helena was not one to mince words. She would say exactly what she thought no matter the consequences. It was one of the reasons the two got on so well. Rebecca was very much the same.

Her other sisters were a bit more, well, flighty. They never spoke what they thought, choosing to let their friends form their decisions for them. She had two other sisters, both not quite of marrying age. She loved them dearly, but they were utterly exhausting to be around.

Rebecca could only pray Helena's mind would be swayed once the pair settled in and grew more accustomed to the town and its people. From what she had spied of the town so far, the town was a bustling ranching down. She had spied people of varying race, color, and perhaps even religion. That last one was more of an assumption really. They seemed to care very little of what was considered fashionable. They chose to wear more practical clothing given the near insufferable heat that had settled across the area.

The men she had come upon were either already married or those whose ages would not allow them the opportunity to wed. Rebecca thanked the Lord above for such a thing. Marriage had never been something she particularly cared for or even desired. There had been not one man in Virginia, upon learning of her determined will and her habit of always speaking her mind, that had not fled in the opposite direction or had sworn she would change when her belly grew round with their offspring.

The door to the small room opening rather suddenly, snapping Rebecca back into reality. A portly older woman stood in the doorway. She could see the confusion upon the woman's face. Her eyes travelled between the two, wrinkled lips pursed in a look of disapproval.

There's...there's two of you?" The older woman inquired; her confusion clear. Her eyes dropped to Helena's rounded stomach.

"I know this is quite unexpected, Mrs....?"

The lady stood a bit taller, "Mrs. Lachlan. I am the former schoolteacher, the one you are here to replace."

Rebecca knew from the brief bit of correspondence that had taken place that the older woman did not willingly relinquish her position. She had been given no choice in the matter. She had grown far too old to handle what the position demanded of her. On more than one occasion, she had been caught sleeping whilst the students did whatever they wanted. Parents had made complaints. She had been stripped of the title and had been allowed to teach under supervision until a replacement could be found. Rebecca was that replacement.

Rebecca stepped forth, "Mrs. Lachlan. It is a pleasure to make your acquaintance. It will be a difficult task to fill the space left behind by your dedication to these students, but I intend to do my best."

Her small bit of flattery seemed to work. Mrs. Lachlan grew red in the face, a soft smile creeping back to her lips. Her eyes were still mostly focused on Helena, "And who might you be my dear?"

Helena offered her hand, "I'm Helena Dubois…Rebecca's sister."

"My widowed sister." Rebecca interjected, "Alas, her husband perished some months ago and I insisted she travel to your fair town. The doctors insist the fresh air will due her good."

From the narrowing of her eyes, the way her lips pursed, Rebecca knew Helena did not relish the idea of being introduced in such a fashion. Rebecca could not risk the former schoolteacher deciding she was a bad fit for the position and voicing her concern to the majority of the town. She could easily be removed from her position.

"Oh, you poor dear." The older woman crooned, laying a knobbed hand upon her sister's arm, "I lost my husband when I wasn't much older than yourself." Her gaze dropped once more, "I did not have a child to occupy my time." She beckoned them both, "Come. This place will not do for someone swollen with child. I shall find you better accommodations in town. Rebecca, your class awaits downstairs. Fear not, I shall take care of your sister as if she were my own."

"I am in your debt." Rebecca assured.

Something in the glint of the older woman's eye let her know that she would surely collect on such a debt.

CHAPTER 2

Rebecca was not accustomed to such heat. The room in which she was designated to teach did not have so much as a fan to keep it cool. The windows were open to allow the soft breeze inside but, alas, it was not enough. She regretted the heavy wool dresses she had brought with her from Virginia. She'd brought only her simplest of clothing which, in this small town, made her stand out even more. The students marveled at the dazzling shades of green and blue that adorned her dress, inquiring without end where she had acquired the string of pearls that hung about her neck.

By the end of the school day, some hours later, Rebecca's entire back was coated with sweat. Her auburn hair clung to her face in a most unattractive manner. The students quickly departed save two little boys. They pace just within the door, occasionally peeking out. Rebecca frowned, approaching the two boys.

The two boys immediately ceased their horseplay, watching her approach with caution. She knelt, "Have your parents not come to collect you?"

She found it odd that just the two would remain. The others, parents or not, had fled the schoolhouse the moment school was over. One boy playfully shoved the other, "My brother here 'as a crush on you, Mrs. Holt." The older one teased, ignoring Rebecca's question for some odd reason.

Her gaze shifted to the younger boy. He refused to meet said gaze. An embarrassed red flamed his cheeks, his body shifted from foot to foot. Rebecca did her best to fight the smile that rose to her lips, "It's actually Miss." She corrected the eldest boy. His name was Henry if she was not mistaken. He was the loudest of the two from what she had seen. And he was quite the little troublemaker.

She fell silent a moment, doing her best to figure out a way to handle this situation. She couldn't have one of her pupils having a crush on her, no matter how small it may be.

"Connor. Is what your brother says true?"

The shy little boy mumbled something she couldn't quite make out. It was clear that the whole situation was utterly embarrassing to the little boy. Sighing, Rebecca brushed her fingers through the small child's unkempt hair. He was filthy.

"I'm quite flattered, if that is the case Conner. Alas, I'm afraid I am a bit too old for you. Is there not a younger girl, perhaps one closer to your own age, that you may fancy a bit?"

Conner seemed to think of this for a moment before a soft grin spread across his face, "Elizabeth is nice."

"Well now, how about you focus all that attention on little Elizabeth then? I'm sure she'll appreciate it."

Conner grinned from ear to ear now. He no longer seemed embarrassed about being outed. He took a step forward, flinging his arounds around Rebecca's neck. She had never been hugged by a child, so this certainly was something new for her. She allowed the boy a moment or two longer before prying his arms from her.

"So, how come you not married, Miss. Holt?" Henry asked rather abruptly.

"Henry." A stern voice echoed from behind them before Rebecca could react. She stood, turning to face the source of such a commanding voice. Her lips parted, jaw nearly dropping when she spied the tall, burly stranger standing a few feet away. The man must have used the back door to enter as she had not seen him arrive.

The two boys backed away. If not for the hint of amusement in the man's eyes, Rebecca would have thought him a stranger to these children. With nothing more than a jerk of his chin, he had the children running in fear of him. They darted out the way this stranger had come to where she now saw a wagon awaited them.

"My apologies, miss. My nephew tends to speak without thinking." He spoke after the children could no longer hear him.

"As do most boys his age, I'm afraid. Wisdom comes with age."

"Aye, that it does." He extended his hand, "Travis Wilson, at your service."

"Rebecca Holt." Her hand slid into his grasp. Despite her better judgement warning her against such thoughts, she could not help but marvel at the way his rough skin felt against the softness of her own fingers. She was unaccustomed to the way his skin bit into hers. He was clearly a hardworking man. He did nothing to hide the appreciative gaze directed towards her.

The silence stretched on for ages…or so it seemed. It probably lasted seconds at most. She snatched her hand from his. If he was offended, it did not show. He plucked the hat from his head, fingers sliding through his thick mane of long dark hair. There was another long period of awkward silence before he spoke again.

"Pardon the intrusion but I find myself wondering the same thing as our young Henry."

She lifted an eyebrow, "You mean why I have yet to settle down and find a husband?"

If her forwardness had any effect on him, he did not show it. His lips curled into a smirk. His dark eyes appraised her a moment before he finally nodded, "Aye. You hit the nail on the head. A woman like you shouldn't be hard-pressed to find a man willing to settle down with you."

"Well, Mr. Wilson, to be perfectly honest, I've never found a man willing to accept me as I am. Most men I meet want a housewife, someone to bow down to their wishes and desires. I refuse to do so. That somehow makes me undesirable to most. And you? Is there a Mrs. Wilson?"

He smiled broadly, "No woman has managed to tame this beast. I like my life just the way it is to be honest. I've no need for a wife."

Rebecca nodded in understanding, "Your family is happy with this?"

"Oh, absolutely not." He laughed, "But they have finally come to terms with it."

Rebecca's heart sank a bit. Though it was nice to have a conversation that did not lead to the eventual assurance that, one day, her views on marriage would change, it saddened her to know that her own family would never accept her reluctance to wed.

Travis seemed to notice. The subject was immediately dropped. The pair stood there for a few moments longer, chatting on the weather and on how the boys were doing with school.

 "Well, I suppose I should be getting these boys home. Their momma and daddy will be wondering where they are." He tipped his hat, sliding it back onto his head, "Same time tomorrow, Miss. Holt?"

She bit back a smile, "I look forward to it, Mr. Wilson."

Perhaps it was the way he spoke, or the way the desert heat rolled across her skin, but Rebecca felt an intense desire to kiss the man standing before her. He gazed upon her with such longing, she knew he felt the same. Her heart bounced around her ribcage as he drew closer. His hand lifted, fingers brushing a loose strand of hair from her face.

"Rebecca!" Her sister's loud gasp snapped her back into reality. She drew back. Helena stood in the doorway; eyes narrowly focused on Travis Wilson. "You will withdraw your hands from my sister, sir."

To his credit, he said nothing. His hand did drop back to his side, "I'll leave you to it then." He addressed Rebecca, "G-day miss." He tipped his hat in Helena's direction before departing the small schoolroom.

"What are you thinking, Rebecca?" Helena hissed once he was out of earshot, "Rumors spread quickly in a town this small!"

Rebecca rolled her eyes, "We were simply talking. Nothing more, nothing less."

"See to it that it stays that way."

CHAPTER 3

T ravis Wilson was a notorious bachelor. No matter how many women had attempted to sink their claws into him, none had succeeded. He was the sort of man Rebecca knew she should avoid at all costs. Or so Helena declared. The eldest sister always was on the protective side when it came to Rebecca. She just did not wish to see the young girl hurt by placing her affection on the wrong sort of man.

Rebecca had no intention of falling into bed with Mr. Wilson or anyone else for that matter. She found it quite insulting that her sister would think her capable of such outlandish behavior. Besides, the schoolteacher had far greater things on her mind than men. That's what she told herself anyway. It didn't matter the way her heart raced each time Mr. Wilson sauntered into the school room. He was always late in picking the boys up. His father, a Mr. Nate Wilson, picked the boys up most days, thank the Lord above.

That afternoon was no different. Mr. Nate wandered within the school in search of his boys. Alas, it would seem he had decided to bring his brother along. Rebecca felt that same prickle of heat against the back of her neck, the same flutter within her chest as he made his approach. She hid it well. Setting her lips into a disinterested line, she refused to make eye contact.

"The boys are outside." She commented, fingertips rifling through the stack of tests littered across her desk.

One of the men, she couldn't be sure which, cleared their throat. Rebecca was forced to remove her eyes from the papers lest she seem rude. Travis leaned against her desk, palms splayed, gazing upon her with a smirk. His brother was nowhere to be seen. He had undoubtedly ventured outside to collect the boys.

"Mr. Wilson." She greeted.

He cocked an eyebrow, "Miss Holt." He replied with just the tiniest hint of sarcasm.

Rebecca bit back a smile of her own. He was incorrigible, "What can I do for you?"

He didn't answer immediately. He pulled away from the desk, fingers rifling inside the lining of his shirt. A frown touched her lips. What on earth was he searching for? After a few moments longer, he finally produced a small piece of parchment which he promptly slid across to her.

"Consider yourself invited." He commented with a wink.

"Invited to what?"

A grin appeared on his face, "Oh, you'll find out soon enough."

"Time to go, Travis." His brother called from the door.

"Hold yer horses!" He hollered back. His eyes never left Rebecca,

"So? Can I tell my parents to expect you?"

The back of her neck turned beat red, something she could easily attribute to the sweltering heat that filled the almost airless room. This was the very thing she had left Virginia to escape. Fingertips lingering on the still sealed parchment, she could only imagine what it contained. She shuddered at the thought of being shoved into a room with other women, forced into small talk and talk of marriage.

"I-I shall consider it." She finally relented.

Her answer was enough. His smile reached from ear to ear as he withdrew from her desk, "Your sister is invited as well. 'Tis a simple event." His eyes grazed her from, "No need to dress fancy or anything."

Her head dipped into a slight nod, "Understood. Now, if you don't mind, I have quite a bit of work left." She motioned to the pile of papers still on her desk, "These won't grade themselves."

"I'll leave you to it then."

Only once he was gone did Rebecca allow herself a moment to breathe. She leaned back into her chair. She covered her mouth with the palm of her hand, shaking her head slightly. After all these years, Rebecca had thought herself immune to the effects of men. Years of being barraged by marriage advances, of being told she'd never be complete without a man to rule over her and a babe on her hip, she had done everything she could to prove them wrong.

Of course, perhaps this attraction was simply in her head. He had given no inclination of wishing to know her further than the professional relationship they seemed to share. She was his nephew's teacher…nothing more, nothing less. Or, at least, that is what she told herself.

Her eyes roamed to the still untouched piece of parchment. Curiosity getting the best of her, she snatched it up. Prying it open, she scanned it. Her lips twitched into a frown. It would seem the Wilson's were hosting some sort of gathering. The invitation did not specify the sort of gathering nor what would be expected of her.

Though she had not agreed outright to attend, she knew already the choice was no longer hers. The moment her sister spotted the invitation, Helena would insist that the pair attend. She would state how it was only proper. Then again, it would be a good opportunity for her to get to know the members of the town. She had been busy getting settled into her new life, she had yet to interact with the town members except for the parents of her students she taught.

The rest of the afternoon passed without disruption. Rebecca was able to finish grading the papers within a reasonable amount of time. She locked up the classroom door, turning to prepare for her ascent to her room. She found the steps blocked by none other than Travis Wilson himself.

"Mr.…Mr. Wilson. To what do I owe the pleasure?"

He didn't speak a word. In two broad steps, he reached her. His hand buried itself in her locks, tearing it away from the bun that held it in place. The musk of a hard day's toil in the fields swept over her, drawing her closer. Their lips met.

The slam of a door yanked Rebecca from her dream. She bolted into a sitting position, blinking furiously. She hadn't even realized she'd been dreaming. Helena stood there; arms crossed over her chest with a look of disappointment.

"I've been awaiting your return for several hours now. Dinner will be cold by now."

"Do forgive me, sister." Rebecca blushed, moving to gather her things.

"Are you well?" Helena inquired, taking note of the blush currently rising to her cheeks.

"Very well, thank you." Rebecca replied a bit too fast.

Helena lifted an eyebrow but said nothing. Instead, she turned her attention to the paper that lingered on the edge of the desk. Before Rebecca could snatch it away, Helena lifted it from the desk. Her eyes scanned it, a giddy smile suddenly appearing on her face.

"Oh! This is just what we need!" She squealed, "Please tell me you accepted this gracious invitation."

Rebecca snatched it away, "Of course I did. It would have been rude of me not to." And, just like that, the young schoolteacher found herself roped into yet another event she held no desire for.

CHAPTER 4

Helena had insisted they bring a covered dish. The pair strolled down the dirt path that led to the Wilson's Ranch. They are not the only ones currently on their way to whatever gathering the pair have been invited to. It appeared as if the entire town had been invited. Rebecca glanced over at her sister. The eldest girl could not contain her glee despite the toll such heat was having upon her. She could see the sweat pooling just beneath her bonnet, the way her cheeks filled with color.

Rebecca herself wasn't much better off. She had dressed in a looser fitting gown, one made of cotton instead of wool. Her hair hung down her back in a braid instead of its usual style. Her sister had refused to dress in anything she did not deem proper for a young woman. She had conceded to Rebecca's urging that she at least abandon her dull dresses the color of a dark storm cloud. She wore a dress just a tad darker than a rose in full bloom.

The ranch was larger than she had anticipated. Even from this distance, Rebecca was able to spy a few heads of cattle. They passed beneath a large sign with the name "Wilson" etched into the wood with bold letters. Children darted between them, far from the grasp of their parents. Things…were different here than in Virginia. She had noticed this the moment she had stepped foot into the small yet bustling town. Only now did she see the true difference.

It was a freer existence. Children could be children instead of being prepped for entering society in a proper manner. Girls could attend school instead of being shoved into tight dresses and paraded around men almost twice their age. Of course, Rebecca wasn't fool enough to believe such things didn't occur here as well. It just seemed the girls had more choice in the matter.

Social standing seemed a bit different here as well. She was unable to distinguish between servants and their masters. She had yet to meet one person that even had a servant. In her home at Virginia, there had been quite a few servants. They were never allowed to mingle with those above them like this. Rebecca had disagreed with this but, alas, it was just the way things were done. Ever since the abolishment of slavery, the wealthier still refused to work their own lands or manage their own houses.

As the pair entered along with the rest, Rebecca was greeted with a rather embarrassing sight. Travis Wilson stood off to the side, surrounded in a nearby field by bales of hay. He was in a state of undress, wearing nothing but a pair of muddy trousers. A lopsided grin appeared on his face as he caught sight of her. Heat rose to her face. She quickly averted her eyes.

Rebecca, under normal circumstances, was anything but shy. She was already twenty, the sort of age where one outgrows childhood fancies and embarrassments. Travis, despite doing nothing that could be considered improper, had somehow managed to wiggle his way past her defenses. Just the sight of him cause her knees to tremble. She would never admit to feeling such a way of course. It would be her little secret.

"Good morning!" A voice greeted.

Two people, one man and the other a small fragile sort of woman, stood not too far in front of them. Nate Wilson and a dark brunette stood off to the right. Only Travis seemed unbothered by their presence as he continued to toil in the field. A few of the other young girls giggled incessantly, each attempting to catch his eye with a swirl of their frocks or a flutter of their handkerchiefs. He ignored them save a dazzling smile before his back turned.

The event turned out to be something they held quite regularly. There were special games designated for the children as well as more adult conversation. Helena fit in without a doubt. Rebecca stood off to the side, content to simply watch without becoming involved.

"You seem less than pleased to be here." His voice sent a flutter through her abdomen. She took a sip of her tea, offering him nothing but a shrug of her shoulder.

"Tis not what I expected is all."

He stepped beside her. He had chosen to finally don a shirt. But, alas, he left it half buttoned. She could still manage a small peak of skin had she but inclined her head. She stared straight ahead. They stood in complete silence, each watching the other people in attendance. A few of the other girls her age, and some younger, stared daggers at the schoolteacher. She knew they felt jealous.

She didn't know how to tell them there was nothing to be jealous of.

"You've yet to make a play." He finally spoke.

Rebecca furrowed her eyes, finally looking upon him, "Pardon?"

His eyes sparkled with amusement, "By this point, most girls would've thrown themselves at me."

"You mean like earlier?"

His grin broadened, "Aye."

Rebecca scoffed, "I've no intention of 'throwing' myself upon any man."

"Oh? Not even if I were to tell you that, one day, all that you now lay eyes upon will one day be mine?"

"What of your brother? Will he not inherit anything?"

"He will, of course. I wouldn't dream of denying him a part of our parent's property. But with me being the eldest, I shall inherit the main portion of the family business."

Rebecca could not help the laugh that slid from between her lips. It took both by surprise, "Oh, Mr. Wilson. I have no interest in your wealth or in what you may inherit in the future. I am quite content to live my life as it is…which I do believe I have already told you before."

He grinned, "Aye, you did. But ya know, things change. When that conversation first took place, we knew very little of each other."

"True. But my answer remains the same." Helena had disappeared from view, giving her the perfect chance to make an escape, "Now if you will excuse me, I must see to my sister now. Good day."

Rebecca hurried off through the crowd. She did not make it far. His calloused fingers curled around her elbow. "Mr. Wilson...!" She bit back her indignant cry.

"Calm yourself, woman." Came his response, "There is something I need to discuss with you in private."

She shrugged off his grip, "I am perfectly capable of walking by myself."

Rebecca knew she should turn him away, refuse to go anywhere without an audience with this man. Despite her reservations, she found herself trailing after him. He led her from the gathering, despite the eyes that followed. Rebecca cared little for town gossip. Let them think what they would. Nothing improper would occur between them.

They ended up at a rather large shed a fair distance from the gathering. There were no spying eyes, no whispering voices that followed. Travis came to a stop, allowing her a moment to catch up before he cracked the door to barn opened. Something told her this was a mistake. A voice inside screamed that she should turn back. But, alas, she did not. She ventured into the darkness with Travis following.

CHAPTER 5

Rebecca's heart thumped against her ribcage. There was very little light within the barn. She squinted her eyes to see. It was to no avail. Crossing her arms over her chest, she turned to face Travis. She opened her mouth but before she had the chance to speak, he was upon her. His palms scrapped against her cheeks, his mouth covering her own.

She let loose a muffled squeal, hands rising with the intent to shove him off. Instead, she found herself melting into him. Her back hit something solid. His hands lifted, fingers yanking her hair out of its braid. Her squeals of disapproval had shifted into moans. Her lips moved with his, her body opening itself to him. He took full advantage.

Before things could progress further, he pulled himself from her. His palms moved to both sides of her, pinning her against the barn wall. "I've been wanting to do that since I first laid eyes on you." He grinned.

Her hand connected with the side of his face. Now that the initial shock of it all had worn off, Rebecca was furious with him, "how... how dare you!" She went to hit him again. He caught her wrist midair, a lopsided grin still plastered across his face.

"I didn't hear you complaining." He chuckled. "You seemed to rather enjoy it."

Her cheeks reddened once more, "It will not happen again."

He pressed himself closer, "Oh? You sure of that?"

She wasn't. Every part of her ached to feel his hands upon her once again. His face lingered, hot breath washing over her. He smelled of hay and whiskey. It wasn't long before she found herself in his arms once more, lips wandering over her bare skin. She knew they should stop, that she should tell him no.

"We...we can't..." She managed to find her voice, "Tis not proper..."

His shirt already discarded on a nearby haystack, her hair an utter wreck, she knew they had passed the line of what was and what was not considered proper a few heated embraces ago. They both wanted what the other was willing to give. Rebecca knew if she lingered in his arms for much longer, she would give in and find herself no longer a woman innocent of a man's touch.

Travis would not be denied. His mouth continued, moving from her neck to depths no person had ever gone. Her fingers curled in his hair for just a moment before she found the strength to shove him away. He blinked for a moment, brows knitting in confusion.

"I-I said no." She breathed.

He cocked an eyebrow but said nothing. He snatched his shirt from the hay, sliding it back on. "Very well." He was angry. Instead of showing this anger, he pulled her back against him, lips hungrily devouring hers, "I look forward to making you mine. You'll deny it, of course. But, one day, you will give in."

Before Rebecca could argue, Travis disappeared from the barn. Rebecca stood there a moment, staring into the darkness. She couldn't even see enough to fix her hair back into its proper state. She did the best she could before venturing back outside. She blinked against the harsh light.

"Rebecca! There you are." The woman she had seen standing at Nat's side came huffing towards her, "The baby is coming."

Rebecca's lips parted in shock, "Oh…oh dear!"

The woman patted Rebecca on the shoulder, "Do not worry. A doctor is on his way. He shall be here shortly." She offered Rebecca her arm, "Walk with me? Your sister is at the house. It isn't a far walk."

Rebecca frowned but looped her arm within this stranger's. They walked in silence for but a moment, "My brother in law is quite taken with you."

Her cheeks reddened, "I don't- "

"Tis too late to deny it. I saw the way he looked at you."

"Nothing will come of it. I've no desire to wed."

The woman giggled, "Who said anything of marriage?"

"I- I do not understand…"

"No one would think less of you for satisfying your womanly desire for the man."

Her ears burned, throat tightening. Perhaps no one would…save for Rebecca. Just the thought of allowing a man to bed her without even the safety of the marriage bed made her skin crawl. She could only imagine her life. Travis would lose interest in her and then what? She risked the possibility of having children with a man that at any point could simply up and leave.

"Are...are you suggesting that I should bed a man and risk the possibility of falling heavy with child just to sate my own person desire?"

"Travis is not a man to shirk his responsibility." The woman shrugged, "Should such a thing happen, I am quite sure he would save you the embarrassment of such a fate. He would no doubt marry you before the babe's birth."

Rebecca withdrew her arm from the woman who looked quite perplexed, "What you are suggesting, ma'am, is simply horrid."

"You wouldn't be the first to obtain a husband through such tactics."

Rebecca turned from the woman she knew to be Nate's wife. She had grown quite fond of Nate over these last few weeks. He was a kind man, a decent man. Did he know the twisted thoughts that wandered through his wife's brain? Or did he share them?

A scream echoed from somehow before her. The scream belonged to her sister. She hitched her skirts, darting towards the sound. She found herself bounding up the steps of a two-story house, flinging the door open. A woman pointed her to the upstairs bedroom. She took the steps two at a time. She found her sister sprawled against a covered bed, a woman kneeling between her open thighs. She arrived just in time to witness the birth of her niece.

"Rebecca!" Helena sobbed as the woman placed the screaming babe in her waiting arms, "it's a girl!" She smothered the blood-stained infant with kisses.

Rebecca joined her sister, forgetting everything but the beautiful sight of her newborn niece. Her fill her heart with both sadness and joy. She knew this was a moment she would never experience for herself. She would never know the love of a child the way her sister would. Rebecca would lather all her affections on the tiny one, intent of providing the little girl with anything and every-thing she would ever desire.

CHAPTER 6

Rebecca hovered just outside the door. They were stuck. The doctor had given strict orders that Helena was not to be moved. He feared for her health. The birth had proved to be quite taxing on the young woman. The lady of the house, Agatha Wilson, had generously given them both a room. How could Rebecca explain her dilemma?

Travis did not live in the main house. He had built his own quaint cottage about a half mile down river. The same with Nate, his wife, and their two boys. They lived on the opposite side of the river. Eventually, the main house would pass to Travis. If he denied his birthright, then Nate would inherit it. Still, Rebecca still could not believe she was relying on the kindness of strangers.

Rebecca was not the sort of woman to readily accept help from others. She preferred to do things herself. But, alas, given their current situation, there was no other option but to accept the offered assistance. Nate had even offered to chauffeur her to and from town each morning. She and the boys would arrive to the school together. It was quite uncommon for the teacher to arrive with the students but there was not one person in town that did not know of their current dilemma. Surely, they would understand.

For the moment, Rebecca could do nothing but focus on her sister and newest member of the Dubois family. Helena had named her Josephine, Josie for short. Her and her dearly departed husband had settled on that name just before his death. They hadn't known of her existence then, but they had each agreed on the name should they ever have one of their own.

Peeking into the room, Rebecca smiled. Helena had finally managed to settle the screaming babe. Both were resting comfortably now. She considered moving the infant into the soft cradle that Mrs. Wilson had so graciously provided but thought it best not to disturb the sleeping pair.

Her stomach growled suddenly, reminding her she had yet to eat that day. She nibbled on her lower lip. She could not bring herself to bother the lady of the house for anything further. Perhaps she would find something in the pantry that did not require cooking.

Holding a demi lit candle between her fingers, she crept downstairs. It was dark outside. She assumed the rest of the house was settled in for the night. Alas, they were not. As she hit the bottom of the stairs, she was forced to bite back a startled cry by the suddenly appearing silhouette of a person.

"I did not mean to frighten you dear."

It was a person Rebecca did not recognize. The person stepped forth, the light from her candle washing over the stranger's face. It was a woman. Her face appeared familiar, but she could not place her. Rebecca took a step back, holding the candle between them.

"What business do you have here?"

The woman chuckled, "I've more right to be here than you."

"Alison?" A soft, almost frail voice echoed from down the hall.

"Coming!" She shouted back, not once taking her eyes from Rebecca, "Travis is mine. I've had my eyes on him for far longer than you. I will not lose him to some little trollop." The woman sneered before turning on her heels.

Rebecca stared after her, blinking in surprise. A frown touched her lips. Her stomach no longer rumbled. Her brief encounter with the girl known as Alison had left her with a bitter taste in her mouth and very little appetite. She needed a bit of fresh air.

Snatching an extra shawl from a hook that dangled just behind the front door, Rebecca wrapped in around her shoulders before strolling out into the crisp summer night. She abandoned her candle. The moon provided more than enough light for her to see where she was going.

She didn't travel far. There was a lake she had seen earlier that day, one she had never gotten the chance to look at up close. She perched along the river's edge, peering down at her reflection. Part of her ached to be home. The other part knew she would never have been fulfilled. She would have been forced into the box of a "proper" young woman. She would be married by now, no doubt, hidden away in a loveless marriage instead of pursuing freedom.

Rebecca never imagined she would find a man worthy of her affections, a man whom did not seek to change her in any way. Then again, just because Travis had yet to speak ill of her chosen profession, didn't mean he wouldn't. Even if by some miracle of God, the pair did choose marriage over freedom…. what would that future hold for either of them?

She would not abide infidelity. She would not be one of THOSE women that knew of their husbands' affairs and let them continue. She would sooner be a widow like her sister than allow a man to take advantage of her in that sort of way. Then again, she had not seen Travis show even the tiniest bit of affection towards another woman. Well, unless that girl Alison counted.

She inhaled sharply, shaking her head. Here in the darkness, it was easy to think of such things. Of course, she would never voice such thoughts to anyone. Helena had far greater things on her plate and, if she chose to mention Travis in her letters home, she knew her parents would insist that he was not a "proper" man to focus her attentions on. It would evitable lead to her parents attempting to find her a suitable husband…and she would not go through that again.

"It's quite late for a stroll."

He appeared from the darkness without so much as the crunch of grass to announce his arrival. She swiveled slightly to face him. "I was in need of some air."

He nodded, "I see." His eyes stared out over the surface of the lake, "I fear I owe you an apology."

"Oh?"

"I should not have kissed you in such a manner." He continued to explain, "It was quite ungentlemanly of me."

"Indeed, it was."

They stood there a moment, the silence stretching between them. When he spoke again, it would seem all was forgotten, "How is your sister fairing?"

"Quite well given the circumstances. The babe is healthy."

Out of the blue, bells began to ring. On the distant horizon, a blaze could be seen reaching into the sky. Rebecca's jaw dropped, "Oh goodness! What is that?"

His face went firm, "We must return to the house." His hand dropped between them, grasping her fingers in his own. For the first time in her life, Rebecca allowed a man to lead her.

It took them but a few moments to arrive back at the house. Travis' father was already out of the house. A buggy sat in the middle of the yard, a large stallion at the head. Without a word, Travis climbed up to join his father. Nate was not far behind.

"Wait! I'm coming as well."

"This is no work for a woman." Nate replied, "Tis far too dangerous." He was quick to explain lest Rebecca take offense at his words. She didn't.

"I've some experience with first aid."

Travis spoke, "She's right. We'll need all hands of deck for this one." He reached his hand down to her, "Allow me?" And, despite her better instincts, she did.

CHAPTER 7

There was little to be done by the time the trio arrived. The house was completely engulfed. A family of four stood just out of the flames reach, staring in abject horror as their home turned into ash. No one was gravely injured. Rebecca treated the wife and one of the small children for some burns. The little girl, she couldn't have been more than eight, clutched a charred doll to her chest. Her face marred with soot, she did not speak a word. Rebecca dipped a cloth in the water bucket at her side, gently washing the soot from her face. She recognized the little girl. She wasn't in her class, her parents didn't believe in schooling girls it would seem, but she knew the girl's eldest brother.

"It's okay dear. You're safe." She cooed.

The little girl shivered but said nothing. Suddenly, the father appeared. He stumbled towards them, his words nothing more than a collection of unintelligible mutterings. He was quite intoxicated. His fingers wrapped around the small child's arm, snatching her away from Rebecca. The little girl screamed, wrenching from her father's grip. She tucked herself behind Rebecca, clinging to her skirt.

The father reached for her again. Rebecca smacked his hand away, "She does not wish to go with you."

"Listen 'ere whore…" he sneered, "That there be MY child. Go…go bear your own bastards."

"You will control yourself!" Rebecca chastised, "The child has been traumatized enough without your drunken ramblings."

By this point, the pair had caught the attention of more than a few people on sight. No one came to Rebecca's aid. The man standing before her was known for his temper. He did not take kindly to a woman telling him what to do.

"I've half a mind to teach you some manners…" He snarled, arm lifting. Rebecca braced herself.

Travis was there before the man could take more than a few steps forward. He placed himself between them, "I would think twice about assaulting a woman in MY presence Joseph." He warned.

The man called Joseph jabbed a finger against the center of Travis's chest, "This be MY land." He hiccupped, "I'll be damned if a woman- "

The man didn't get a chance to speak further. Rebecca heard the crunch of bone, saw the blood dripping from his face as Joseph collapsed to the ground. Travis swore, shaking his hand. No one said a word, "Someone come collect him. He'll have a broken nose but perhaps he'll think twice about threatening a woman."

"I did not need your help." Rebecca spoke.

Travis shot her a look. Her lips pressed together. She knew that look. It was one her father had given her many times whenever she spoke out of turn or in a way that displeased him. She folded her arms over her chest. She knew she should thank him for intervening, perhaps show a bit of gratitude, but she could not.

It took hours for the flames to die. By the end, Rebecca was thoroughly exhausted. She sat in the back of the buggy, the small girl whose name she now knew to be Agatha curled in her lap. The sweet child had been through a great ordeal that night and she was exhausted. That made two of them. Rebecca could barely keep her eyes from closing.

A sturdy hand shook her awake, "Rebecca."

"I'm awake…" She half yawned.

Travis smirked but said nothing. He pulled the whimpering child from her lap. Rebecca did not like the idea of letting the drunkard of a father anywhere near that child but, alas, the choice was out of her hands.

"The mother and children will be staying with family until their home is rebuilt." Travis remarked as he handed the child back to her mother, "Do not fret. The child will be safe."

"Her father is not worthy of that title."

"Worthy or not, he is still her father." Travis shrugged, "He's a right to his children, Rebecca."

Rebecca hadn't the strength to argue. Nate climbed into the buggy, positioning himself in the driver's seat. Travis did something…well, unexpected. He hauled himself in the back of the buggy, tucking himself in the small area between Rebecca and the side of the buggy.

He motioned her closer. Rebecca found herself leaning against him, eyes closing once more. She wasn't sure how long she slumbered. When she woke, they were back at the house. Travis slid from the buggy, swooping her into his arms. There were murmurs from the others, perhaps a look or two. Travis ignored them all. He carried her into the house.

When Rebecca awoke later that day, she was surprised to find herself wrapped in covers. She had no memory of climbing the stairs, no memories of tucking herself into the bed. Curtains had been drawn over the window to keep the light out. She shifted into a sitting position, blinking in confusing.

The scream of a babe drew her attention. Pushing the covers back, she stood. She had taken two steps when the babe's cry was replaced with a long, drawn out, scream. The hairs on the back of her neck stood up. She knew that scream. Bunching her skirts, she darted for the door.

When it opened, Travis stood in the opening. His eyes were bloodshot from a sleepless night. His face appeared pale. He did not allow her to pass, "Your sister- "

Something was wrong…something was horribly, horribly wrong. She pushed him aside. He let her. She flew down the long, narrow hallway towards the room where her sister resided with her newborn baby girl. Nothing could have prepared her for the scene that greeted her.

Helena lay on the bed. Her chest rose and fell but she would not move. Mrs. Wilson clutched her sister's child to her own chest. When she saw Rebecca enter, she made her approach. She hands the fussy infant to her.

"I caught your sister attempting to smother the child."

Rebecca's jaw dropped. No...that could not be right. When Rebecca attempted to approach her sister with the infant, Helena immediately began to scream, "I don't want it!" Tears streamed down her face, "Get that abomination away from me!" She screeched again.

Rebecca backed away. The child now cried in unison with her mother, tiny fingers grabbing at Rebecca's blouse. It sought milk. Helena would not settle, not until the tiny girl was out of her sight.

"Why is she acting in such a strange manner?" Rebecca inquired, doing her best to settle the hungry babe.

Nate appeared, holding a bottle of milk, "Tis goat's milk." He offered. The infant took the bottle without complaint.

"It happens, unfortunately," Mrs. Wilson explained, "We do not know why. Some women are just not equipped to be mothers."

Nate's wife appeared beside her husband, "Here. Let me."

Rebecca refused to hand her niece ofto such a person, "If my sister is unable to mother this child, then that responsibility falls to me...and only me. I'll be her mother."

CHAPTER 8

The shrill scream of a babe pulled Rebecca from her sleep. Once again, she stumbled into the small room that housed said infant. The crib she rested in had been generously donated by a member of the town. Helena still refused to nurse the poor child so, alas, she was forced to rely on weekly donations of goat's milk and cow's milk.

Josie did not appear to relish the idea of drinking the liquid. She fought Rebecca every feeding. Eventually, the small infant's hunger would get the best of her and she would suckle from the bottle. Over the course of the past week, the infant had grown increasingly fussy. Rebecca could not settle the girl no matter how hard she tried. Josie needed her mother.

Rebecca did not trust her sister to be near the fragile baby. With the assistance of The Wilson's, her sister had been offered a room at the local inn where Rebecca would visit her daily. She would bring Josie with the hopes that at the very least, Helena would agree to nurse the child. She never did. She wouldn't even so much as look at the child.

Rebecca hovered over the crib, palm of her hand rubbing Josie's chest as she screamed. Part of her ached to scream as well. Nothing she did seemed good enough. Tears streamed down her face as she lifted the unsettled infant. She rocked her in a gentle motion, all the while patting her on the back. She still insisted on crying.

"Oh, what is the matter little one?" Rebecca cooed.

She was at a loss with what to do. She had never held an infant before her niece had come along much less been forced to deal with the constant crying. Surely such behavior was not normal?

She felt the babe's head, searching for a fever. There was none. She felt a perfectly normal temp. She shifted the baby to her other arm. She was about to lay the infant down when there came a knock at the door. Her eyebrows pinched together. Who on earth could be at her door at such an hour?

She carried the still screaming infant to the front door. She was not expecting the stranger that stood on the other side of the door. It was a heavy woman with quite a...well, a large bosom. Travis stood at her side. The woman took one look at the crying infant and quickly scooped her away before Rebecca could react.

"Josie is in good hands." Travis assured, sensing her bubbling anger before she had a choice to speak. He entered without permission, shutting and locking the door behind him. "She's here to offer her services as a wet nurse. She just had a babe of her own and has plenty to spare."

Rebecca felt those words as one would a slap to the face. She never dreamed the day would come when, like many of the affluent families she had grown up around, she would need a wet nurse. Of course, that was for an entirely different reason. She never dreamed she would ever have a babe of her own. Granted, Josie was not hers by blood. There was still a bond between the two. Rebecca would protect that sweet child with every breath in her body...even if it meant separating her forever from the woman that had given her life.

"What is she expecting in return?" Rebecca spoke after a few long moments of silence

Travis shrugged, a broad smile threatening to split his cheeks "As far as I know, she expects nothing in return."

Rebecca snorted in disbelief, "I find that hard to believe."

Girls like that were always expecting something for their services. Rebecca had witnessed it firsthand more times than she dared speak of. They would swoop in under the pretense of wanting to help or needing the pay the position promised. She recalled one family. The mother had just undergone a hard labor and was unable to feed her child. This woman stepped in and, not only took over the feeding of the baby, she took over the home. Before said woman knew what was happening, her husband had cast her into the streets.

Travis seemed quite amused by her distress. Instead of reprimanding her, he stepped closer. His fingers lifted, pushing a loose strand of hair back into place. His next words sent shivers down her spine. "If I did not know better, I would think you were jealous."

"I haven't the faintest idea to what you are referring."

That was a lie. She would never admit the burning desired she harbored for Travis...she didn't need to. He knew without her having to speak a word of it. Something in the way his gaze softened as their eyes met told her that he understood her reluctance to admit to such feelings. She had gone through most her adult life with the notion that she would never find happiness with a man. She had been perfectly fine with such a future. That had changed the moment Travis Wilson had waltzed his way into her little school room that day.

"Miriam and I are friends. Nothing more, nothing less. Besides, she just so happens to be married and quite happily from what I've been told." He spoke softly though she hadn't asked about the woman at all.

Rebecca did her best to swallow the hint of relief that swelled in her chest at the news that the young lady in her bedroom was married and harbored no attraction of her own for the rancher,

"Can she be trusted?" She finally asked.

Travis did not hesitate with his answer. "Aye. I'd trust her with my life. She adores children."

Rebecca went to answer but, alas, a yawn interrupted her thoughts. She fought against it but to no avail. Travis cocked an eyebrow for a moment.

"When is the last time you slept?"

She shrugged, "Josie refuses to settle. I've done what I can." In that moment, Rebecca realized she no longer heard Josie's piercing cry, "Perhaps I should have considered a wet nurse sooner. She seems content."

"She would not be the first babe to prefer the milk of a woman over that of an animal." Travis assured her, "Come. You should rest."

Rebecca was exhausted. She knew Travis was right. She shouldn't allow the stranger brunette to be alone with her niece, but the couch beckoned to her weary soul. She allowed Travis to escort her to the makeshift bed. She slid beneath the thin cotton sheet. In her hurry to answer the door, Rebecca had forgotten that she wore nothing but her dressing gown. The material was thin.

Heat rose to her cheeks. She prayed the material was not so thin as to allow Travis a peak of what lay hidden beneath. Her eyes lifted for a moment. His eyes were not on her face but travelled lower. Desire flashed in his dark eyes, the palm of his hand rubbing the stubble of his chin as if to silence something that threatened to leave his mouth.

"Sleep tight, Rebecca." He purred. His face lowered, lips just barely brushing against hers.

CHAPTER 9

R ebecca awoke the next morning with a sense of dread. It was something she could not explain. Josie slept peacefully for the first time in days. The young lady named Miriam lay in her bed, passed out after what she could only assume was a long night. She considered waking the young lass but decided against it. Miriam had been a godsend despite her previous reservations. The least Rebecca could do was let the girl sleep.

Travis was nowhere in sight. He had left the girls in peace. There was no school that day, so Rebecca decided to cook the young lady in her bed a nice breakfast before she awoke. It didn't take long for the sizzling bacon to wake Miriam. She appeared in the small kitchen, cradling a happy yet awake Josie.

"Morning, ma'am." Miriam spoke.

"Would you care for something to eat?" She offered, scooping the eggs and bacon into a small plate, "Tis the least I can do."

"I really should be getting home," Miriam sighed, "My husband will be wondering where I am." Her eyes dropped to the offered plate, "But I suppose a few minutes longer will not hurt."

Rebecca took Josie from Miriam to allow the girl to eat. Josie babbled happily away, tiny fingers pulling and twisting at Rebecca's hair. Miriam said not a word, not until she finished every bite from her plate. Only then did she push from the table, her eyes directed at Rebecca.

"It is a fine thing you are doing, miss." She nodded towards the infant cradled in Rebecca's arms, "Not many women your age would be willing to care for an infant they themselves did not birth."

Miriam was right of course. Such an act would be looked down upon in Virginia. Even if said child was family, it was considered taboo for the mother to simply abandon their child to another family member. Unwanted children were generally deposited at an orphanage or workhouse. Rebecca could not, nay, would not do such a thing to her niece.

"She is family." Rebecca explained, "I could not abandon her."

Miriam nodded, a soft smile rising to her lips, "I can see why Travis fancies you."

Heat rose into Rebecca cheeks. She said nothing. Travis spoke about her to others. The rumors, if they hadn't already, would start soon. She would not be able to cross the street without whispers following her...the same as they had in Virginia. Of course, those rumors had been of a different sort altogether. She would need to speak to Travis.

"Travis is not the sort to spread rumors, if that is what you are wondering. He is not accustomed to women of your sort...the kind that aren't easily swayed by his charm." Miriam continued to speak, doing her best to alleviate her fears, "I have never seen him light up the way he does whenever your name is on his lips."

"It was never my intent to capture his attention."

"But, alas, capture it you have. 'Tis up to you what you will do now that you have it."

"I have never been in such a dilemma." Rebecca confessed, "Most men, once they find out I've a mind of my own, often want nothing more to do with me."

Miriam laughed, "Travis is NOT that sort of man at all. He's put off by frivolity and the way most girls throw themselves at him. He isn't wealthy by any means but, around these parts, he is what most would consider a catch. He is set to inherit the family business. Cattle ranching is big in these parts."

"So, I've been told."

Miriam cocked an eyebrow, "You know of his impending inheritance and, still, you refuse him? My, my, that is impressive indeed."

"I've no time for marriage." Her chin dipped towards Josie, "between teaching and this little girl, I do not have the energy to spare."

"Travis loves children."

Miriam was beginning to make Rebecca regret allowing her to stay. It would seem the girl was insistent on pushing the pair together, whether it was something they wanted or not. If Miriam picked up on her frustration, she did not show it. She lifted herself from the table, brushing the tiny bit of crumbs from her dress.

"Shall I nurse her once more before I leave?" Miriam offered. "I-I can take her for a bit if you would like? I live just around the corner."

Rebecca sucked in her lower lip. She knew she shouldn't. She was not sure if she trusted Miriam or not. Travis certainly seemed to trust her. Perhaps that was enough. With some reluctance, she allowed Miriam to pry Josie from her arms.

"I've some errands to run. I'll be but a few hours." Rebecca offered as explanation, "If I do not come fetch her, you can simply come here and await my return."

Miriam nodded though her attention seemed rather focused on Josie. Rebecca stood rooted in place whilst Miriam carried little Josie from the small room. A faint smile tugged at her lips. Josie seemed rather fond of Miriam. The feeling appeared mutual. Travis had said that Miriam had just had a little one so that begged the question...who was watching her infant while she'd been here the whole night? Her husband, presumably, had kept watch over her newborn.

Slipping into one of her recently acquired cotton gowns, Rebecca headed out. She had told Miriam she had errands but, really, only one held her attention. She needed to speak to Travis...to tell him that there was nothing between them once and for all. He mustn't speak of her to anyone lest someone get the wrong impression of her.

CHAPTER 10

I t did not take long for Rebecca to travel to the Wilson Ranch. At first glance, it appeared no one was home. Then, from the corner of her eye, she spied a flash of light coming from the barn to her left. Taking a sharp inhale of the dry summer air, she slowly approached the massive building. Sure enough, Travis was just inside. His back was turned so he did not see her approach.

He did not wear a shirt. Rebecca came to an abrupt stop a few inches within, watching with utter fascination as the shirtless Travis heaved bale after bale of hay into the bed of a wagon. He took a moment of pause, snatching a bit of cloth from the railing nearby to wipe the sweat from his brow.

Rebecca could not breathe. She stood rooted in place, unable to move. Her eyes scoured his bare skin, heat creeping up the back of her neck. She should announce herself, look away, something… anything. She couldn't. Her mouth turned to desert. Her heart thumped against her rib cage. She began to feel lightheaded, as if she might faint.

He chose that moment to finally turn. His lips curved into a smirk, eyes devouring her in the same fashion hers had him only a moment ago. He abandoned the bales of hay, choosing to lean against the railing that separated them.

"Well, this is unexpected." He chuckled lightly, "To what do I owe the pleasure?"

Rebecca cleared her throat, folding her hands before her as she stepped towards him, "Miriam seems to be under the impression that you fancy me in some way."

Travis cocked an eyebrow, "And this is a problem because....?"

"It is a problem because such rumors could ruin what little reputation I have in this town."

His grin grew wider, "Pardon me for saying so, but I didn't take you as the kind of woman to care what others think of her."

Her cheeks turned scarlet, "I don't but given my position as schoolmarm, I have to consider my actions carefully. I cannot afford to have the reputation of a woman of ill repute."

Travis ran his palm over his face, head shaking with slight amusement, "I did not tell her any part of what transpired in the barn that day, Rebecca. Besides, Miriam is a trusted friend. She would never spread rumors."

"Forgive me if I do not take you at your word. I've none many a people that, though they claimed to be above such things, were at the forefront of spreading vicious lies.... even if it was unintentional."

His chore now forgotten, Travis hopped the railing with ease. Rebecca took a step back to put some distance between the pair. He was not having that. He closed what little distance remained, forcing her back until she hit the side of the barn. His palms caressed the wood on either side of her head.

"What is it you DO desire of me, Rebecca?" He inquired, "You say you want nothing to do with me but here you stand."

"I only came to say- "

"To say what? To say that no one should know of us. I thought there was no us, Rebecca. At every turn, you refuse to acknowledge this...this fire between us."

"That is a lie." Rebecca hissed. She shoved him back, "Do not presume to know me, sir."

"That's just it, Rebecca." Travis sighed, "I don't know you. I don't know you at all. But I would like to. I've never held even the slightest interest of marriage but there is something about you... something that makes me reconsider that viewpoint."

Rebecca blinked. Was he saying what she thought he was saying? Surely, he was not offering himself in marriage to her. The two were barely acquaintances. They were practically strangers.

"I've told you before, Travis, that I have no interest in marriage."

"I do not believe you, Rebecca. I think you've told yourself that enough times that you've come to believe it. You've resigned yourself to being alone because you assumed all men were alike... that none of us could look past your outward beauty to the person you are beneath. I would never change you, Rebecca. Surely you know that by now?"

"You're already trying to change me, Travis." She whispered, "You talk of marriage when we are but strangers. You only desire to have me in your bed." She accused.

"Aye, I make no secret of that." Travis agreed with a shrug of his shoulders, "I would like nothing less than to have you writhing beneath me, to feel your supple skin beneath my touch."

And there it was…the true reason he was offered himself to her. Her lower lip quivered, indignation bubbling to the surface. He wanted a whore in his bed, not a wife. Under the law, there would be a difference, but he cared no more about the brain she possessed than all the others.

"I will not be your whore." Rebecca spat.

"I never-" He began to speak.

"You are like all the rest." Rebecca accused, interrupting him. She threw her hands in the air, "You don't desire to know me at all. You just want the pleasure my body can give you."

"Travis, darling, is that you?"

The woman from before, the stranger that had instructed her to stay away from Travis, appeared in the doorway of the barn. She wore nothing but a thin shift, thin enough that Rebecca could see the delicate outline of her bare breasts through it.

Travis stared at the young girl, blinking in what appeared to be confusion. The girl, whose name she did not know, stared at Rebecca. Anger flared in her emerald shaded eyes for a moment before she made her way over to where Travis stood. The palm of her hand caressed his bare chest.

"I've been waiting for you, lover."

Rebecca had heard all she cared to hear, "I'll leave you to it, then."

She turned, storming from the barn. She didn't care to see any-more. A small part of her realized that her jealousy was silly given what they pair had just discussed. The other part of her was in utter disgust by how she could have allowed herself to ever have feelings for that man. She should have known the sort of man he was. Never again…never again.

CHAPTER 11

A letter had arrived. Rebecca stood inside the postman's office, staring down at the parchment she held between trembling fingers. She knew from the expert penmanship that the letter was from her mother. She had not written since the birth of her niece, so mother did not know that Helena refused to care for her own child. She did not know that the motherly duties were being divided between herself and Miriam, the woman who had so graciously offered to be her wet nurse without expecting any-thing from her.

Dearest Daughter,

It warms my heart to know you have found happiness at long last. Though I dreamt of a different life for you and your sister, I can find comfort with the knowledge your sister is there to keep watch over you.

Father has taken ill. I fear he will not last the summer. I do not relish the idea of speaking such words in a letter, but I do not intend to visit now or ever. I do not ask that you and your sister return. I would never ask you to abandon a happiness so quickly found.

Rebecca could read no further. She crumbled the letter up, shoving it down into the pocket of her dress. A single tear rolled down her cheeks. Mother's father, Rebecca's grandfather, was not long for this world. It was not news to her. He had been in poor health even before she had left.

Rebecca still felt great sadness for his upcoming demise. He was a gentle man that never had a word of ill for anyone. He had been the only one to support her choice of coming here. Not even Father had agreed that this was the right choice for her. He was willing to support her desire not to marry so long as she at the very least remained in Virginia.

Helena needed to know. With a sigh of resignation, she departed from the small building. The inn where Helena currently resided was not far. She passed a local farmer's market. She stopped for a moment to browse their wares. Helena was not eating as she should so Rebecca thought, perhaps, a bit of fresh goods would do her some good. Alas, she did not see anything worth purchasing. Due to the severe drought, the amount of fresh produce was dropping by the day. Those that were plucked from the soil were small and hardly worth the price they were being sold for.

As Rebecca made her way down the cramped aisles of produce, she stumbled upon a pair of older women deep in conversation. They spoke in hushed tones, glancing around every few moments to ensure they were not overheard.

"Quite scandalous, is it not?" One of them whispered.

"Oh indeed. What sort of woman refuses to care for their own flesh and blood?" The other woman gasped, placing her hand over where her heart should have been.

Rebecca's entire body froze, ears burning. She knew in that moment they were speaking of her sister. No other woman in town had given birth recently. The women continued their malicious talk, each comment worse than the last.

"Poor Rebecca should just rid herself of the burden." The other woman remarked, "How will she ever find herself a husband?"

Now, the women clearly did not see her standing a few feet to their left or else they would have seen the look of utter horror that washed across Rebecca's face. They were insinuating that Josie was a burden instead of the gift she considered her to be.

Before Rebecca could speak a word, another person joined the group. Half hidden behind a large pillar; she could only stand on in awe.

"You ladies should be ashamed." The man hissed, his voice soft enough for only the three of them to hear.

"Mr. Wilson…" One of the women began in a feeble attempt to explain herself.

"That woman is nothing but a saint, taking in her sister's child with no thought of herself."

The bolder of the women was not so easily intimidated, "You fancy her. While else would you come to the aide of such a woman? I've heard she is not as pure as she makes herself out to be."

Travis was silent a moment. When he did speak at last, his tone had changed. There was more bite to his words, "You will hold your tongue, woman. I have nothing but admiration for that woman.

"I've heard the rumors." The bold woman sneered once more.

"Lies." Travis assured her, "There is nothing between Rebecca and I except a modest friendship."

"Alison declared otherwise. I know for a fact she caught you two in a…"

"You will not finish that sentence," Travis growled, "I've never put hands on a woman before, Suzannah, but so help me god if you so much as breath another lie about Rebecca, you will force my hand."

Rebecca swallowed. The name Alison sparked some recognition but, alas, she could not place it. It was clear the stranger held so animosity towards her. Why else would she spread such horrible lies about her? The woman and her friend did not speak another word. Rebecca heard them shuffle away a moment before a pair of fingers tucked themselves in the crook of her elbow.

"We should speak." He spoke loud enough for her ears only.

"I do not think that wise." Rebecca argued, thoughts turning back to the last time they had spoken in private.

"There is nothing between Alison and I. I do not know why she was at the house the other day, but I can assure you it was not by my invitation. I scolded her sharply after you left and have not seen her since. I can only assume therefore she is spreading lies about the two of us. She seeks to ruin you most of all."

In that moment, Rebecca suddenly realized why the name seemed so eerily familiar. "She was there….the other night when my sister almost..." She couldn't bring herself to speak of what had almost been done that night. She cleared her throat, "She instructed me to stay away from you as if she had some previous claim."

Travis blinked, lips tilting into a frown, "Well, I can assure you that is not the case. Alison and I grew up together. Her father used to work our fields. I consider her a friend...or, well, I did. As of late, she's gotten this notion that she and I should wed. Nothing I say will convince her otherwise I'm afraid."

Rebecca did not speak. She could think of nothing to say. There was such sincerity in this voice that it was hard not to believe him. The way she had acted earlier caused her great shame. She was not the sort prone to jealousy...especially over a man she had repeatedly told herself she held no feelings for.

"I see." Rebecca pursed her lips, "It would seem I owe you an apology."

His dark eyes sparkled with amusement, "I'll settle for a kiss." His fingertips brushed against her cheek, sending shivers down her spine.

"I...I cannot." She murmured, taking a small step back to put some distance between them, "I am on my way to visit my dear sister. I mustn't be late."

He said nothing. Though it pained her to do so, Rebecca turned her back.

CHAPTER 12

Helena did not look well. The eldest of the two sisters welcomed Rebecca into the tiny room that she had been provided but the warmth in her face was no more. Her cheeks were hollow. Heavy bags hung beneath her eyes. Even her clothing appeared too big for her withering frame.

"It is nice of you to visit." Helena sighed.

"I am only sorry I could not come sooner." Rebecca offered, "I've been busy with little Josie and with my teaching."

"How.... how is she?" Helena inquired, stumbling over the words as if she struggled to even speak of her own child.

"She's quite well. She grows bigger with each passing day. I've had to hire a wet nurse as she was not taking to the goat's milk."

Helena averted her eyes, guilt entering her dull and lifeless eyes, "Oh, sister. I never...I never meant for this to happen." A tear rolled down her cheek, "She reminds me of my dearest Edward. The moment I looked upon her face, I saw him."

Rebecca lay a reassuring hand on Helena's shoulder, "Little Josie is welcome in my home for as long as you need it, sister. You could visit her if you like."

Helena bit on her lower lip, "I-I do not think that wise, sister. They told me what I almost did. That I almost…. almost murdered my own child." She sounded on the verge of tears.

"Think nothing of it, Helena. Tis already forgotten."

"I have no memory of it!" Helena declared. She gripped Rebecca's hands in her own, "I would…I would never harm a child. Surely you know this?"

"Aye….I do."

The rest of the visit was spent in virtual silence. Helena tired with ease, eventually retiring to her bed before Rebecca had even left. She prepared her sister a meal, tucking the covered container into the ice chest before making her departure. It hadn't been the visit she was anticipating.

Helena had barely even asked about little Josie after the first few moments. Rebecca could not understand her resistance to mothering the small infant. Perhaps it was because she had not lost what Helena had. Perhaps it was simply too difficult for Helena to gaze upon the baby that mirrored her dead lover.

Rebecca paused in the doorway, gazing back at her sister once more. Helena stood at the window, staring down upon the bustling town. She did not look like herself. Shutting the door behind her, Rebecca hurried from the inn. Being unable to help her sister just when she needed it the most broke her far worse than she would ever admit.

For as long as she could remember, Helena had always been there.

At the numerous galas and dances where she had stood to the side, alone, her sister had been there. She'd refused other's requests to dance just to keep Rebecca company. The two were closer than any of their other siblings.

Rebecca returned to the schoolhouse. Miriam was nowhere to be seen. Lips tilting into a frown, Rebecca stood by the winding staircase that led to her room. She tapped her foot impatiently. Where was she? She hadn't been gone that long. With a sigh, Rebecca decided to travel to the young woman's house. She wasn't quite sure where she lived. Miriam had told her of the blossoming yellow flowers that grew wild by her front door. Alas, many of the homes in the area seemed to possess the same flowers.

She stopped a man passing by, "Pardon me, sir. I am looking for a woman by the name of Miriam."

The man cocked an eyebrow, "I'm afraid there are a few women of that name. Do you have a last name?"

Miriam had hold her, but Rebecca could not for the life of her remember what that name was. She thanked the man and hurried on her way. Her only other option was to return to the schoolhouse and wait. She never expected what awaited her.

The schoolhouse was aflame. Smoke poured from the roof, completely engulfing the room upstairs along with all her possessions. Rebecca could do nothing. Others quickly gathered and a waterline was set up. It was far too late. The flames refused to die. The others seemed to realize this as well, but no one wanted to give up.

Rebecca could not breath. The very reason she had come so far from home was gone now. What would she do? What purpose would she serve now? Tiny fingers tapped her arm. A few of her students stood behind her, their innocent eyes staring up at her with confusion.

"Do not fret, children. We will.... we will just move our classes. Tis nothing to fret about. All will be well."

She didn't believe that for a moment. From the crowd, two familiar faces made their approach. Miriam and Travis fought their way through the thickening crowd that had gathered. Miriam looked pale. She brought with her that small precious bundle that, now, she had no place to keep.

"Oh Rebecca!" Miriam wept, "What happened?"

"I do not know. I arrived here, expecting you to be waiting. I went searching but was unable to find your home. By the time I returned, the school was engulfed."

Travis's lips tightened, "This was no accident."

Both women looked at Travis. "What do you mean?" Miriam questioned, "Surely no one would do such a thing on purpose? Rebecca could have been inside!"

"I think that was the point."

Rebecca shuddered. To think that there was someone in town with such hatred towards her that they would seek to do away with her was utterly horrifying. Her gaze shifted to the sleeping baby in Miriam's arms. Her heart sank. What would become of them now?

"I'll have my husband make up the second bedroom for a guestroom." Miriam announced, "It will be crowded but we shall make it work."

"I couldn't possibly ask that of you, Miriam."

The woman waved a hand, "Tis nothing. I'm glad to help."

Though she appreciated the gesture, Rebecca could not help but hesitate. Miriam had expressed nothing but kindness in the weeks since she had first become Josie's wet nurse. Still, she did not much about the woman. She only knew that she was married, happily if the rumors were to be believed, and had two children of her own.

Rebecca knew she had no other choice. It was either that or a room at the same inn where her sister was currently residing. There was a possibility that they would be full, and she would still end up with no place to go. With a sigh and a nod of her head, she silently agreed to what Miriam was offering. She had no clothing, no money, nothing. Everything she had owned had burned in the blaze.

"We shall make this work." Miriam assured.

Travis had barely spoken a word. His eyes remained focused on the still smoldering remnants of the school. "I will see to it that whomever is responsible is apprehended at once."

CHAPTER 13

R ebecca stood amongst the chaos. Miriam's house was in a constant state of disarray. Apparently, Miriam's house was where all the little ones would go whilst their parents worked the fields or did whatever they did to earn money for their home. Miriam did not seem to mind. With babe on hip, she made her way through the swarm of children camped out in her front living area towards the kitchen.

Rebecca helped where she could. Miriam graciously allowed her to hold class outside on her front lawn where all the children could attend, both boys and girls alike. Time passed quickly. The person responsible for the fire had yet to be found despite Travis's best efforts. He and a few men from the village were in the process of rebuilding the school. It would be a few more months still before she could move back.

Travis made regular visits to the home. Though suspicious of his intent at first, Rebecca began to warm to his presence. He never spoke of marriage, never pressured her into anything she did not feel comfortable with. There were a few nights where the pair would exchange heated kisses in the dark of night, tucked behind the house far from view of others. It never ventured further than that.

Miriam's husband was not so kind as Rebecca was led to believe. He resented her presence in his home. She would often find his eyes following her, a sneer on his face when he thought no one saw. If Miriam noticed, she spoke nothing of it. There was nothing but affection between them from what Rebecca had seen. She did not blame him for not wanting her there.

The children would leave at night, leaving just the three adults and the three children. Josie flourished in that house. She grew from a sickly infant to a blossoming, inquisitive child. Rebecca could see the love Miriam bathed that girl in. It warmed her heart. One particularly warm afternoon, Rebecca left Josie in Miriam's capable hands whilst she went to visit her sister.

Helena's health had made some improvement, so Rebecca was quite surprised when she entered the small room only to find Helena shoving the last remaining articles of clothing into a sack clock. She met Rebecca's gaze, lips tilting into a frown.

"I am returning to Virginia. I have written mother. She agrees it is for the best." She took a moment to compose herself before speaking again, "I should like to take Josie with me. I think it's important she be around family right now."

Rebecca's heart dropped, "What of me? Am I not family enough? I've poured every ounce of myself into the raising of that child over this last six months. Now you're just going to take her? You cannot. I will not let you."

Helena's eyebrows pulled together in a look of utter confusion,

"She is not your child, Rebecca. She is mine."

"You threw her away!" Rebecca accused, her heart shattering. She had not realized the level of affection she'd felt for Josie until that moment, "How can I know you won't do it again once I am no longer around to stop you?"

Helena said nothing, "I've spoken to the sheriff. If you do not hand the child over when I come to collect her, I won't have a choice. I'll have you arrested."

"I am your sister!" Rebecca could not believe what her sister was saying. After all these years of impeccable loyalty, this is what it came down to? "Helena, please…" Her voice broke, "Do not take her from me."

"Do you think I want to?" Helena scoffed, "She is my daughter, Rebecca. I love her. Despite…despite what happened shortly after her birth, I cannot just abandon her."

Rebecca could not breath. Her entire body began to shake, hot tears streaming down both cheeks. Helena refused to look her in the eye. She simply continued stuffing bits of clothing into the sack.

"You could come with us." Helena spoke at last, "The school is gone. You've no reason to stay now."

She was wrong. Despite her promise to never do so, Rebecca had fallen for a man. The idea of leaving Travis behind was not something she could even think of doing. She had a choice now. She could depart this town and be in her niece's life or she could stay and run the chance of never seeing little Josie ever again. Neither was ideal.

Helena saw the indecision written across her face, "You love him, don't you?"

Rebecca swallowed hard, lips parting to answer. No words came forth. Helena offered a kind smile.

"I wish nothing but the best for you sister. I hope you do reconsider your views on marriage. Travis would make a fine husband. You could have a child of your own."

How could Rebecca explain to Helena that she considered Josie hers? Though she had no right to think such a thing, she could not help it. For six months, Rebecca had cared for that babe. Rebecca did not wish to miss a day of her life. If Helena took her, she would never get to hear that child utter her first word, see her take her first steps.

Helena was in no state of mind to be caring for a child. Besides, Josie was far too young for such a dangerous trip. There would be roaring rivers to cross not to mention the heat. Josie was better off here with her and Travis. Rebecca was sure of it. Now how to convince her sister that Josie would be far safer here?

"She's too young, Helena. She will never survive the journey."

Helena paused, eyes lifting to appraise her sister. Her lips tilted into a frown. Rebecca knew her sister was no fool. She would see through the lie. To be fair, it wasn't a lie really. The journey was far too dangerous for a six-month-old child. Of course, she had known infants far younger than that to have survived such a trip. She had spoken it out of desperation.

"Rebecca, Josie is coming with me and that is final. Nothing you can say will dissuade me. My mind is made up."

Rebecca could not bear to stand there and watch as Helena prepared to snatch Josie from her grip. She fled the room, hurrying to the one person she knew would offer her comfort in that moment.

Travis exited his home shirtless. He took one look at Rebecca's tear stained cheeks before ushering her within his home. Rebecca knew it was a mistake, but she entered, nonetheless.

CHAPTER 14

W hat had she done? Rebecca hurriedly fastened the last of her buttons, refusing to gaze upon the rumpled sheets behind her. She didn't need to. The dull ache between her legs was evidence enough of what had transpired just a few hours before. She could hear Travis moving about in the kitchen. She wished to be dressed before he returned.

"What's the hurry?" Travis spoke from the doorway. He held two plates of food in his hands. "Josie is safe with Miriam." He set the plates down on the side table, moving to curl is arms around her waist. His lips caressed the crook of her neck. His hands moved up, fingers catching hers.

"This was a mistake." Rebecca murmured, "I-I should never have come here." She shoved him away.

"I thought this is what you wanted." Travis returned; his tone laced with hurt.

Rebecca covered her face with both palms. She didn't know what she wanted. She'd been hurt and in need of comfort when she'd showed up at his door. She had never expected things to go so far. In the moment, there had been nothing she'd wanted more than his body against her own. But now in the cold brutal light of day, she realized what a horrible thing she had done.

"My sister is taking Josie and leaving for Virginia." She blurted out, "That is what I came to tell you last night."

Travis made his approach. Forefinger caressing the underside of her chin, he forced her to look at him, "If I had known, I would never have- "His gaze dropped, "I took advantage of you."

Rebecca shook her head, "It is I that took advantage. I used you. I was hurting and in desperate need of a distraction."

His lips curled into a half smile, "I was happy to oblige."

Her forehead rested against his chest, her fingers intertwining with his own, "How can she do this?" her voice broke, "I love that little girl as if she were my own."

"Can you not convince her otherwise?" He purred, lips touching the top of her head.

"I tried. Her only suggestion was that I return to Virginia with them."

"And you do not want this?"

She lifted her chin, "I cannot leave. I owe it to this town to finish out my teaching term."

His head tilted. His hand left hers, moving to cup her face, "Is that the only reason you do not wish to leave?"

Their lips met, tongues dancing. God, he tasted divine. Before she quite knew what was happening, her legs were wrapped around his waist. He pinned her arms above her head as he lowered her to the bed. She wanted him more than ever. He shared the desire.

Rebecca did not know how many times that day he took her to bed. She relished in every moment of it. When the sun set on that day, Rebecca knew what she must do. She forced herself from the bed. He did not wake. She dressed quickly, departing before he could awake to stop her. She did not get far.

"I knew it."

Rebecca gasped, whirling to face the delicate female voice that had spoken. It was the woman known as Alison. She propped herself against the house wall, lips pulled into a sneer.

"You are nothing but a whore."

"I haven't the time for this." Rebecca rebuffed her, "Travis has no interest in you, Alison. Tis better that you realize that now before you get hurt."

Rebecca turned her back to the girl. Had she known just how volatile the young woman was, she would never had exposed herself like that. The woman dug her nails in Rebecca's scalp, yanking her back with more force than Rebecca could have thought her capable of. She screamed.

"He is MINE!" Alison pulled Rebecca down onto the ground, climbing on top of her. Her fingers wrapped around the base of her throat, "He will never love you the way he does me."

Despite her small stature, Alison was quite strong. Rebecca could not fight her off. She thrashed, nails digging in Alison's flesh. It was to no avail, she was manic. She would not release Rebecca. She stretched out her arm, desperately searching for something with which to protect herself with. She wouldn't need it. Travis bolted from the house, having been awoke by the noise.

"Alison!" He declared, masculine arm wrapping around the young woman's waist. He pulled her from Rebecca.

Rebecca rolled to the side, gasping and coughing as the air entered her lungs once more. Travis tossed Alison aside, coming to Rebecca's aide. He never saw the glint of metal as Alison pulled something from her apron. His attention so focused of Rebecca that he never sensed the danger.... not until the blade pierced his side.

"If I cannot have you then no one can." Alison screamed, yanking the blade out with the intent to stab him again.

A gunshot rang through the air. Alison stumbled backwards, blood gushing from a wound in her chest. Rebecca rushed forwards just as Travis crumbled. Ripping a piece of fabric from her apron, she went to cover the wound. His brother appeared, their father following.

"I knew she had become infatuated with Travis." His brother sighed, staring down at Alison's dead body, "I never knew she would take it this far." His gaze shifted to his ailing brother, "We'll fetch the wagon."

Rebecca could do nothing but hold Travis and await the wagon. Travis groaned, chuckling a bit, "No need for tears. I'll be fine." He spoke through the pain.

"This is my doing."

Travis rolled his eyes, "No. Tis mine. I knew she held affection for me. I was flattered, at first. I should have done more to discourage it. If anyone is to blame, let it be me."

"Does it hurt?"

"Only when I breath." He took another ragged breath of air before continuing, "I know how much that little girl means to you. If…if you feel you need to go, then I will not stop you. I will not be the reason you miss out on her life."

"I love you…." Rebecca whispered, finally admitting to him the truth she had been so desperately fighting to ignore.

He smiled gently, "I know."

CHAPTER 15

Two months had passed since Travis had been injured at the hands of Alison. Helena had delayed her journey, long enough for Travis to recuperate. Rebecca had been at his side day and night. The two never spoke of her confession nor of what the future would hold. He knew she had a decision to make. He did not seek to sway her one way or the other. But something else would.

Rebecca had not bled in those two months. She knew nothing for certain, but she held a suspicion that she was with child. She could not bring herself to tell anyone. The shame was too great. She was faced with a far great decision. If she should leave for Virginia, her child would be known as a bastard. He, or she, would be shunned. She faced the uncertainty of even being allowed to remain in her home once it was found out that she was expecting.

She knew Travis would offer to marry her out of duty. She could not ask that of him…not after everything he had gone through to protect her. Rebecca would not ask him to give up his freedom for her. She knew that was the one thing he valued above all else.

The knife had sliced deeper than any of them had first realized. He was not allowed from the bed for fear that the movement would rip open his carefully placed stitches. Rebecca and the others did what they could. Travis did not take to being bedridden well. He felt into a depression of sorts. He refused everyone but Rebecca to aide him. Even then, he would lash out with anger.

His temper was fleeting and never lasted...especially when he could move about the house. He still could not climb the stairs or do any manual labor. The Wilson's had to hire some extra hands to work the ranch whilst Travis was incapacitated.

One day, Helena came for a visit. Rebecca, Miriam, and Josie were in the front parlor. Travis and his mother were in the kitchen. From the firm look on Helena's face, she knew the day had come that she had been dreading for the past two months. Her eyes dropped to little Josie who sat playing with a toy horse that Travis had carved especially for her.

"No." Rebecca said the moment Helena stepped into the parlor, "Please, sister. I beg of you...don't take her."

"I offered you the chance to accompany us." Her eyes drifted to Travis who had wandered into the parlor at this point, "Your choice has been made it would seem."

When Helena reached for little Josie, the girl began to scream. Her tiny arms lifted, fingers reaching for Rebecca. Helena stared in shock as Rebecca scooped the wailing child into her arms. Helena reached for her again. Josie buried her face in Rebecca's hair. She refused to even look at Helena.

"Give her to me. Now." Helena demanded.

"Please, think of what is best for the child." Travis's mother interrupted, "You are a stranger to her."

Helena's face flushed, "I am her mother." She reached for the child once more. Her hands wrapped around the infant's waist, pulling her rather forcefully from Rebecca's grip.

Both she and Josie wept at that point. Helena settled the fussing infant onto her hip, "The offer still stands, Rebecca."

There was nothing Rebecca could do. She knew she could not return to Virginia. With her current condition, she would be even more an outcast than she already was. Rebecca's hand fell almost subconsciously to her stomach before she shook her head.

"I.... I cannot...." She whispered, barely able to speak without sobbing.

Helena's eyes dropped to where her hand rested before lifting. There was a slight twinge of remorse before she looked away, "Very well." She turned. Josie had not stopped screaming at this point. Her tiny face was red, hot tears splashing down her face as she reached for Rebecca over Helena's shoulders.

Travis came to stand beside Rebecca. The pair watched Helena carry the child from the house. Rebecca felt faint. Only Travis's arm tightening around her waist kept her from crumpling. Josie's screamed echoed. Though she was no longer in her line of sight, she could still hear her wails of despair.

The despair did not last long. Her cries grew close one more. Up to this point, no one in the room had spoken expected Rebecca. Now, Miriam rushed to the pained glass windows.

"She's coming back."

Rebecca pulled herself from Travis's grip, rushing out the front door. Sure enough, Helena stood a few feet from the door. Josie wailed. Tears streamed down Helena's face as Rebecca made her approach. She allowed Rebecca to take the child from her.

"She would not stop crying." Helena spoke, carefully wiping a tear from her cheek, "Though she was born of my womb, she is not mine."

Rebecca pulled the eldest of her sisters into a tight embrace, "No matter what, little Josie will know that you are her mother. I will tell her of your sacrifice…that you only wanted the best life for her."

"Thank you."

"You could stay." Rebecca offered, "No one is forcing you to go."

Her gaze dropped to little Josie who not clung to Rebecca's neck. She shook her head, "Tis best that I go. It will not be forever. I never dealt with Edward's death as I should have. I…I need time." Her fingers stroked the side of Josie's face, "I'll be back to visit."

"I'll write."

Helena smiled, "I'd like that." Her gaze shifted to the crowd that had gathered behind Rebecca, "Travis Wilson, you take care of my sister. I best not return her and find her still unwed."

Travis grinned, "I fully intend to make an honest woman out of her."

Rebecca's cheeks turned a brilliant shade of red. When she turned, Travis no longer stood. He knelt in the grass. He presented a diamond nestled into a gold band with emeralds on both sides. It was divine. She couldn't breathe. After all the talk of him never wishing to wed, here he was on his knees presenting her with such a dazzling gem.

Helena did not depart. It would seem she was awaiting Rebecca's answer before making the trip back to Virginia. "Travis…I- "

"I know you said you did not wish to wed, Rebecca. For so long, I thought the same. But, alas, I cannot bare the idea of a future without you in it. I'll never seek to deny you your freedom. You'll continue to teach, and I'll continue to work this land. We'll have as many children as you like…none if that is your preference. Just say you'll be mine."

Rebecca's heart thumped against her ribcage. Her eyes drifted to the people standing about. Each one's face filled with a dizzying array of emotion. His mother appeared on the verge of tears. His father beamed with pride. She knew they desire this for their son…. for them both.

The one thing they did not know was that she already carried their grandchild. Would they look upon her in a different light once they found out? It didn't matter, not in the end. There was only one answer to the question he asked.

"Yes."

CHAPTER 16

The wedding was days away. Helena had chosen to stay until after the two were wed. Rebecca had yet to tell anyone of her condition. Each day, her stomach grew rounder and it became harder to hide. She resorted to wearing more flowy gowns to hide her shame.

She had not allowed Travis to touch her since that day all those months ago. He never pushed the subject. But, alas, once they were wed, what would he think then? She could not keep this secret forever. She stood before the floor length mirror, studying herself within the clear glass.

She cradled her abdomen, lips tilting into a frown. She did her best to picture what their child would look like. Would it be a strapping young man like his father? Or perhaps a delicate flower like Rebecca. There was no way of knowing at this point in time.

"Rebecca..."

Her eyes lifted, catching sight of him in the mirror. Her hands dropped from around her waist, but it was too late. He had seen her secret. He approached her from behind. His arms encircled her from behind, palms caressing her stomach.

"Why did you not tell me?"

Rebecca sighed, "I did not want sway your decision."

His lips curled into an amused of smile, "I would have married you regardless, Rebecca."

"What will your family think?" Rebecca spoke, turning to face him, "Will they think less of me?"

His fingers lifted, forcing her chin up. Their eyes met. He pushed back a strand of hair that had fallen from her braid, "I can assure you this will change nothing."

"He's right, of course." His mother spoke, suddenly appearing in the doorway, "I could not be more thrilled that we are to be grandparents once more." She pulled a silver rattle from the pocket of her apron, "I can finally give you this...now that you've told him."

"Mother.... did you know?"

She shrugged, "I suspected as well. She's been so quiet as of late, so distant."

Rebecca's eyes widened, "You did not say anything."

"I wanted you to tell us when you were ready, dear."

Tears welled in her eyes, "You still would welcome me as your daughter in law despite my condition?"

She nodded, "Aye. I would have welcomed you and your child with open arms even if the two of you hadn't wed." She motioned to Travis, "I would never had scorned a member of this family."

Rebecca was overwhelmed by the woman's sense of duty to her

family. Her arms curled around her stomach. She no longer had to keep her secret. It was as if a great weight had been lifted from her shoulders.

Travis pulled her into a tight embrace, "I am going to be a father."

He said those words with such pride, such contentment. She buried her face in the front of his shirt, allowing her tears to fall forth. He held her, gladly soaking up every single spilt tear. His mother did not linger. She set the rattle down on the dresser and excused herself. The pair were left to their own devices.

He held her close, allowing her to inhale his musky scent. Eventually, they made their way to the bed. Nothing happened. He simply held her. His hand would eventually make its way to her protruding belly. He caressed her skin, humming a soft tune.

"I was thinking Hannah if it is a girl." Rebecca commented, covering his hand with her own, "Isaac if it's a boy."

"I do not care." He murmured, "So long as the child is healthy, we can call him or her whatever you wish."

Rebecca lifted herself onto an elbow, "Are you happy?"

His lips touched hers, "Very. Why do you ask?"

A heat rose to her cheeks, "I do not want you to regret this in the future, Travis. Baby or no, I do not wish to deprive you of your freedom."

A grin rose to his face, "I would gladly sacrifice every ounce of my freedom if it meant having you."

Her fingertips caressed his stubbled chin, "My parents will be at the wedding."

His grin widened, "I'll be glad to meet them at last."

Her hand lowered to her stomach, "I fear how they will react. They do not know I am with child." A tear rolled down her cheek, "I fear they will be most cross."

"If they are, then so be it. What's done is done, Rebecca." Travis did his best to alleviate her fears, "I do not believe they will deny their grandchild if that is what you think.

That was the very thing she feared, above all else, that her parents would cast her aside as their daughter and refuse to accept her child. She would survive but it would shatter her heart to have to live a life without them. Despite the great distance that separated them, she wanted them to be involved in her child's life as well as in josie's life. They both deserved two sets of grandparents.

"They arrive in two days."

He nodded, "That's the day of the wedding."

"I know."

He pulled her to him once more, lips claiming hers. The house was silent, dark as night had fallen. The satin sheet slipped over them, his hands making quick work of her clothing. Rebecca melted into his touch, her own hands disrobing him as well. They were not married yet but, somehow, what they were doing did not seem so wrong. Perhaps because she was already with child, Rebecca allowed him to have his way with her.

It would not be the first time the pair would lie together that night. By the time the sun peeked over the horizon, Rebecca felt her body could take no more. Travis would not relent, bringing her to the precipice of pleasure once more before he too was spent.

When the pair finally awoke, it was far past noon. The rest of the house had already begun last minute wedding preparations. The ceremony would be held there on the property. Travis's mother had insisted. Rebecca wandered out across the grass, watching the hustle and bustle. She had been refused the ability to help due to her being with child. No one wanted to see the child harmed by too much manual labor.

"Rebecca!"

She turned. Mother and father were here. Her eyes widened. She had not been expecting them so soon. She no longer wore a flowing dress. Now that her condition as known, she hardly saw the point. It was clear from the looks of shock upon her parent's faces that they knew. She swallowed, preparing for the argument that was about to ensue.

CHAPTER 17

Mother and father had yet to speak. They sat across her, each taking careful, measured sips of their afternoon tea. Mother appeared pale, her hands shaking as she set her tea down. She refused to so much as look at Rebecca. Helena sat opposite her, little Josie bouncing on her knee.

"I've heard rumors that the schoolhouse was burnt down." Father spoke first, clearing his throat.

"Aye. That was some months ago. The new one is coming along nicely."

Mother could stand it no longer. She slammed her cup down on the table, "Really, Rebecca? Just what on earth were you thinking? How could you shame this family in such a way? I mean, what will those in Virginia think? You are…with child!" She said these last words with such disgust it caused Rebecca to cringe.

"Martha, calm yourself please." Father spoke, laying a restraining hand upon Mother's leg. He focused his gaze on Rebecca, "This man you are marrying, it isn't simply because you are with child? You know you always have a place beneath our roof."

"Aye, papa. I know that." She turned her attention to her mother, "I did not plan this, mother. Surely you know this. Travis is a kind soul and I love him. This child will want for nothing."

Mother's face softened just a bit, "You love him, you say?"

"Aye. And you will love him to, I am sure."

Her gaze searched the practically empty parlor, "And just where is this man of yours?"

"He's out in the fields, tending the livestock. He won't be back till sundown."

"He's a working man, is he?" Father commented.

"He takes pride in his work. He's never been one to simply lay about." Rebecca bragged.

"This ranch…it will be his one day?" Mother inquired.

Rebecca fought the urge to roll her eyes. Of course, that was what Mother was concerned about. Rebecca loved her Mother dearly, but she was never quite able to understand her interest in the finer things of life.

"Yes, Mother. Being the eldest, he will inherit the property. Of course, his intends to half said property with his brother. The two will share equal ownership in the property."

Father nodded, "He is a man of honor."

It would seem Father was more willing to accept the situation then mother. Father would eventually get through to Mother…. or so Rebecca hoped. The rest of the evening was spent conversating about the weather and then Josie. Rebecca and Helena had agreed that is was best to not speak of what had happened upon the young girl's birth. They settled on the version that entailed how sickly Helena was after the birth, of how she could not care for her child and how Rebecca had taken the burden upon herself.

Rebecca did not see it as a burden. In fact, a large portion of her still viewed Josie as hers. But, alas, she had come to the realization that the little girl was not hers. Josie had a right to her mother just as Helena had a right to her daughter. It eased her spirit to know that Helena had changed her mind about returning to Virginia. In fact, it would not be long before Helena married again.

The eldest sister had caught the eye of a local widower named August. He seemed a decent man, though nowhere near wealthy. He grew tobacco a few farms over. The two had begun a delicate courtship, neither wanted to rush as they both had children. August had two daughters a bit older than Josie. His wife had perished giving birth to the twin girls.

Finally, Travis made his way in from the fields. He greeted her parents. The three seemed to get along. Finally, the day of the wedding arrived. Her mother had brought the same wedding dress she had married in. Travis's mother provided the veil. All was set.

"Do you Rebecca take Travis to be your lawfully wedded husband?" The preacher inquired of her. Travis had already spoke his "I do's." It was her turn now.

"I do." With those last two words, Rebecca and Travis were married, and on their way to living their lives together. She couldn't quite believe it, but there he was, standing solidly beside her.

CONCLUSION

Thank you for reading Rebecca and Travis' storey.

I hope you enjoyed it!

Finally, if you enjoyed this book, then I'd like to ask you for a favor, would you be kind enough to leave a review for this book on Amazon? It'd be greatly appreciated!

Just keep swiping and you will be prompted to leave a review for this book.

Thank you.

Kat Lynne

PREVIEW OF 'WYOMING BRIDE'

Chapter 1: Unforgettable Memories

The sound of thunder frightened the young Amelia Taylor as she curled up in the makeshift tent inside her room. It was a stormy night and her mother promised to be with her. She waited and waited until she saw a terrifying streak of lightning sliced through the night sky. She ran to her tent and hid there, hoping her mother would come soon.

"Mother, where are you?" The little girl softly whispered.

"Call my name whenever you are afraid and I will always come." She remembered her mother's reassuring words. Those words gave her the confidence to hold on. She knew that she would be nestled within her mother's warm embrace real soon.

After a while, the door of the little girl's room creaked. A familiar shadow came into view, and Amelia did not need to confirm who it was.

"Mother!" She uttered excitedly as she ran out of her tent.

"Amelia, I love you." Her mother gave her a faint smile before she dropped, lifeless on the floor.

The young girl did not understand why her mother became like that. She slowly walked to where her mother was. She looked at her mother's motionless body. She sat beside her mother and gently poked her cheeks. No response. She poked once more, this time with a bit more force.

The little girl began to panic as she finally noticed her mother's disheveled hair and pale complexion. She began tugging her mother's sleeve as tears fell from her eyes.

"Mother I don't want to play this game. Please stop it." There was no response even when she kept tugging her mother's sleeve. She tried patting her mother's back and discovered that it was drenched with something warm.

She lifted her hand and was about to inspect it when a figure emerged in the doorway. Another streak of lightning flashed and it was enough to illuminate the room. Amelia saw that the stranger was holding a knife. She shrieked at the top of her voice, but the roaring sounds of thunder and heavy rain swallowed her screams.

Terror crept in her heart as she finally understood what had happened. She looked at the stranger and she knew that death was coming.

* * *

"Ahhh!" Amelia screamed as she opened her teary eyes. Her mother's death anniversary was approaching. She always dreamt of that horrific event whenever this day was approaching.

"Amelia!" Samuel Taylor, Amelia's father, came running. Aunt Susan, who helped raised Amelia, followed suit.

Amelia was panting and the terrified look in her eyes could not be concealed. It was obvious that she was only half awake. She suddenly stood up and walked. Her actions suggested that someone was chasing her and she was struggling to get away.

Samuel was deeply pained to see his daughter like that. He knew that it was related to the incident seventeen years ago. Every year, her daughter seemed to return at that exact moment when she was only five years old, cooped up in her makeshift tent waiting for her mother to come.

Every year after that fateful night, Samuel Taylor would witness his daughter going through the same thing. It was much worse during the first few years. He saw how the young Amelia tried to break free from his embrace as he tried to calm her down. She was pounding at his arm and tugging at his hair. She even bit him once so hard that he almost threw her off.

A friend suggested that it might be good to seek a professional's help. Amelia must have been traumatized by what happened that year. The case of Madame Taylor's death remained unsolved. The only witness was the five-year-old Amelia Taylor. At the time, Samuel had decided not to pursue the case to protect his daughter. He was scared that the interrogation could bring more harm than good.

Samuel yanked his daughter's arm and hugged her tight. He called out her name hoping to wake her up completely. "Amelia, wake up!"

As if she was pulled out from the trance, Amelia blinked her eyes and finally woke up from her stupor. She felt familiar warmth from the person hugging her. She hugged her father tightly and sobbed. Father and daughter stayed like that for quite some time.

Every year, on Madame Taylor's death anniversary, Samuel tried his best not to show any sign of weakness to his daughter. He knew that the woman named Amelia Taylor was strong, but he was afraid that the little girl inside that strong woman might suddenly fall apart.

Click here to check out the rest of Wyoming Bride on Amazon.

https://www.amazon.ca/Wyoming-Bride-Western-Historical-Romance-ebook/dp/B07RM69WGL

https://www.amazon.com/Wyoming-Bride-Western-Historical-Romance-ebook/dp/B07RM69WGL

Also by Kat Lynne

Montana Bride

https://www.amazon.ca/Montana-Bride-Western-Historical-American-ebook/dp/B07PS6CRPL

https://www.amazon.com/Montana-Bride-Western-Historical-American-ebook/dp/B07PS6CRPL

Wyoming Bride

https://www.amazon.ca/Wyoming-Bride-Western-Historical-Romance-ebook/dp/B07RM69WGL

https://www.amazon.com/Wyoming-Bride-Western-Historical-Romance-ebook/dp/B07RM69WGL

If the links do not work, for whatever reason, you can simply search for these titles on the Amazon website to find them.

www.ingramcontent.com/pod-product-compliance
Lightning Source LLC
Chambersburg PA
CBHW071924120726
48001CB00005B/1865